John W. King

The Silent Dead

John W. King

The Silent Dead

ISBN/EAN: 9783741180781

Manufactured in Europe, USA, Canada, Australia, Japa

Cover: Foto ©Andreas Hilbeck / pixelio.de

Manufactured and distributed by brebook publishing software
(www.brebook.com)

John W. King

The Silent Dead

THE SILENT DEAD,

OR

ROLL OF HONOR;

Comprising the names of all Soldiers from Muskingum
County, who lost their lives in battle or by
disease, during the War of Rebellion.
Reported to date Jan. 1, 1866.

BY JOHN W. KING,

ATTORNEY AT LAW.

ZANESVILLE, OHIO:
PRINTED AND PUBLISHED BY LOGAN & DODD.
1866.

IN MEMORY OF THE
Fallen Brave.
THEY DIED FOR THEIR COUNTRY.

NOTE EXPLANATORY.

This pamphlet was promised to the people of Muskingum County at the Soldiers' Barbecue, held September 2d, 1865; but its appearance has been delayed in consequence of the retaining by the Government of several of our organizations in the field, whose mortality could not be known until their recent muster out:

In the lists, the greatest accuracy has been aimed at, but to know and record the name of each hero who went forth from the many quiet homes among our hills and throughout the towns, and thereby perished in the cause, has been a work of unexpected difficulty. Instances have occurred where even the mother or the father could not tell whether their missing boy was dead, or what had been his fate.

In addition to the usual work of inquiry, and research into the military records of the various Regiments and Companies, requests have been repeatedly published, through the courtesy of the press, calling upon all to send in to the compiler, lists of names from every quarter of the county, and branch of the service. The utmost limit of time for returns has been granted, and it is hoped that every name is now on the ROLL, there to remain in *shining* honor.

Any inaccuracies or omissions will be as much regretted by the author as by friends of the deceased.

THE DEAD.

It was by mere accident that the present writer became entrusted with the labor of preparing the following ROLL OF HONOR. The idea originated with the welcome that was given to the returned soldiers. In this enterprise our County may claim to be first. No other County in Ohio, or in the nation, has published such a record.

In its preparation the following facts have attracted attention:

The whole number of deaths by battle have been Five Hundred and Eighty-Four. Of these Springfield Township lost Sixty-One, the most of any, and Clay Township Seven, the least number. By sickness and railroad accidents, One Hundred and Seventy. Among the cases of prison mortality we count Forty-Three:—at Andersonville, Thirteen; Libby and Belle Island, Five; Florence, Nine; Macon, Three; Millen, Five; Sallsbury, Two; Charleston, Six.

Our County has bled mortally on the following battle-fields, which include the chief engagements this side of the Mississippi River and the lower Atlantic Coast:

Vienna, Alleghaney, Rich Mountain, Cheat Mountain, Bull Run No. 1, Greenbriar, Cross Keys, Port Republic, Chickahominy, Malvern Hills, South Mountain, Antietam, Corinth, Pittsburg Landing, Fredericksburg 1 and 2, Holly Springs, Stone River, Rappahannock, Fort McAllister, Franklin, Va., Somerset, Ky., Tuscumbia, Port Gibson, Chancellorsville, 1 and 2,

Port Hudson, Raymond, Jackson, Champion Hills, Bull Run No. 2, Gettysburg, Vicksburg, Morgan's Raid, Fort Wagner, Chickamauga, Chattanooga, Missionary Ridge, Lookout Mountain, Kelley's Ford, Culpepper Court House, Knoxville, Strawberry Plains, Orange Court House, Tunnel Hill, Dalton, Pleasant Hill, Wilderness, Spottsylvania, Resaca, Dallas, Kenesaw Mountain, Peach Tree Creek, Atlanta, Weldon Road, Monocacy, Petersburg Mine, Moorefield, Snicker's Gap, Deep Run, Cedar Creek, Franklin, Nashville, Fisher's Hill, Wilmington, Fall of Richmond, Pursuit of Lee.

The graves of our dead heroes are scattered through thirteen different States. Most of them are buried where they fell, and few have monuments to mark the spot.

> "In many a fevered swamp,
>   By many a black bayou,
> In many a cold and frozen camp,
> The weary sentinel ceased his tramp,
>   And died for me and you!
> From Western plain to ocean tide
> Are stretched the graves of those who died!"

On a tablet erected near the graves of the Andersonville dead is the following inscription:

> "Through all rebellion's horrors,
>   Bright shines our nation's fame,
> Our gallant soldiers perishing,
>   Have won a deathless name."

In the first engagement after the fire on Fort Sumter our county suffered a loss. June 17th, 1861, the murderous fire of the rebels on our troops at Vienna, Virginia, was made; and three men, George Morrison, H. Pigram and David Mercer, were mortally wounded. They are buried at Camp Upton, near Washington, like thousands of others, in unmarked graves.

> "But glory guards with solemn round
> The bivouac of the dead."

Sixty-Five regiments and battalions are represented in the Roll of the Dead, from Muskingum county.

Of these, forty-eight are of infantry, eight of cavalry, three of artillery, two of navy and gun-boat, and four regiments from other States of the Union.

In the back of the pamphlet will be found the Commissioned Officers' Roll. It comprises eighteen names. The ranking officers in the list were Major B. G. O. Reed and Major Wm. Edwards. Nearly every one of them died by the bullet.

None of our Colonels or Generals died in the strife. Not a single officer of the One Hundred and Twenty-Second Regiment, from this county, died of disease.

In preparing the following pages, many sad stories have been recited and heard. The lovely boy is gone, and neither friend or parent knows where he rests; no solid wall or hasty fence, even, surrounds his patriot dust, and no stake, board, or better, marble, marks the spot. The battle, perhaps, raged over miles of country, and the dead fell into the hands of the enemy, who hid them in the earth, rather to get them out of sight than to pay a decent respect to a fallen enemy. In this way, painful as it is to fond parents and admiring friends, the blood of our soldiers enriches many an unmarked spot; while the ravages of disease, less to be feared than the prison rigors and punishments of a savage, but determined foe, transferred others to unknown patriot graves. On many of the great battle-fields National Cemeteries have been erected, which, with their monuments, under the care of a grateful nation, will be more enduring than the tombs and cenotaphs of Greece or the Orient.

The Hon. Secretary of War has authorized the Quartermaster-General to send out burrying parties to numerous battle fields, who will disinter the remains of soldiers scattered through the woods and waste lands and bury them in suitable cemeteries. This has been done at Gettysburg, Chattanooga and the Wilderness; of the latter there are two, known as No. 1 on the right and No. 2 on the left.

The laudable design of erecting monuments in the counties to the memory of the soldiers, has been inaugurated, and the enterprise of raising a monument at the capital of the State, to perpetuate the memory of the fallen braves, and also one in honor of Abraham Lincoln, which, while it shall bear witness to his virtues and his worth, shall also "plead, trumpet-tongued, against the deep damnation of his taking off."

These efforts are right, and ought to remind the people of Muskingum County that they have no "pile, or shaft, or marble" erected to the praise of her dead soldiers. Something has been said upon the subject, and it is reported that a commanding and beautiful lot in Wood Lawn Cemetery, will be donated. Argument in favor of this, certainly is not expected. The valor of our soldiers, the right of their cause, and the deliverance of the Republic, appeal by their lonely graves— by their deadly conflicts, and their uncoffined dust, to the hearts of the people, for a home monument, where we can all gather at its solemn dedication, and deposit a copy of this *Roll of Honor* beneath its corner stone, in grateful tribute to their sacred memory.

ADAMS TOWNSHIP.

W. B. Bell, company F, Sixty-Second.
Anthony Gaumer, company F, Twenty-Sixth.
Joseph A. Lydig, company E, Ninety-Seventh.
S. W. Mills, company H, Fifty-First,
David Ross, company E, Ninety-Seventh.
Ezra Ross.
I. N. Steers, company E, One Hundred and Sixtieth
National Guards.
J. J. Stuart, company E, One Hundred and Sixtieth
National Guards.
D. G. Sturtz, company H, Seventy-Eighth.
J. J. Sturtz, company E, Ninety-Seventh.
Christian Sandel, company A, One Hundred and
Second.
James Saffell, company E, Second.

BLUE ROCK TOWNSHIP.

J. D. Austin, company D, Seventy-Eighth.
W. D. Conner, company D, Thirty-First.
Matthew Crawford, One Hundred and Seventy-Eighth.
Marion Dempster, company D, Twenty-Fourth.
John F. Dutro, company I, One Hundred and Sixtieth
National Guards.
Samuel Dutro, company D, Seventy-Eighth.
Perry Echelberry, company F, Forty-Seventh.
Davis Echelberry, company D, Seventy-Eighth.
Joseph Gander, company C, Eighth Wisconsin.
William Hamler, company K, One Hundred and
Twenty-Second.
Albert Hunt, company D, Seventy-Eighth.
William Kinney, company D, Seventy-Eighth.
Charles Kinney, company D, Seventy-Eighth.
Noah Kinkade, company E, Second.
Nathaniel McCann, company D, Twenty-Fourth.
Frank McGuire, company A, Ninth Cavalry.
Josiah McLees, company I, One Hundred and Sixtieth
National Guards.
John H. Nelson, Twenty-Second Battery.
Frederick Osborn, company D, Seventy-Eighth.
John Price, company B, Sixty-Second.
David F. Peairs, company K, Ninety-Seventh.
Joseph Roberts, company B, Sixty-Second.
John Riddle, company D, Twenty-Fourth.
Captain E. Hilles Talley, company D, Seventy-Eighth.
Isaiah White, company I, One Hundred and Sixtieth
National Guards.
Andrew Wallace, company D, Seventy-Eighth.
William Weaver, Ninety-Seventh.
William A. White, company D, Seventy-Eighth.

BRUSH CREEK TOWNSHIP.

David Baughman, company A, Sixty-Second.
Moses Dozier, company K, Ninety-Seventh.
Lewis Crane, company A, Sixty-Second.
William Deiterick, company K, Ninety-Seventh.
Hiram Dozer, Twenty-Fourth.
Uriah McGee, Twenty-Eighth.
Grafton Harrop, company A, Sixty-Second.
Jacob Harrop, company A, Sixty-Second.
William Hamrick, company H, Ninety-Seventh.
James Larrison.
Charles Lucas, company E, Ninety-Seventh.
Josiah H. Lucas, company E, Ninety-Seventh.
Henry Neibel, company E, Ninety-Seventh.
James Prindle, company E, Ninety-Seventh.
John Riddle, Twenty-Fourth.
George Trout, Seventy-Eighth.
Joseph Trout, company A, One Hundred and Twenty-
    Second.
Stephen Woodruff, company A, Sixty-Second.
Newton Wells, company E, One Hundred and Seventy-
    Eighth.

CASS TOWNSHIP.

Jay Adams, company A, Seventy-Sixth.
W. II. Austin,   "   A,   "
Howard Adams, "   A,   "
Benjamin Butler, Thirty-Second.
Andrew Casner, company D, Sixteenth.
Richard Casner, company D, Sixteenth.
William Davis, company D, Sixteenth.
C. C. Lemert, company A, Seventy-Sixth.
John Mills, company D, Sixteenth.
Lafayette Morgan, company G, One Hundredth.
Franklin Monroe, company D, Sixteenth.
J. II. Ogle, company F, Sixty-Second.
Miner Prior, company A, Seventy-Eighth.
Benjamin Palmer, company F, Sixty-Second.
Abraham Robinson, (colored.)
Abraham Spurr, jr., Ninth Cavalry.
Frederick Starner, company F, Ninety-Seventh.

CLAY TOWNSHIP.

Joseph Axline, Ninth Cavalry.
Major William Edwards, Sixty-Second.
David Hetzel, (unknown.)
James E. Kildow, company II, Eighteenth.
James M. Porter, company G, Thirty-First.
Bushrod Patterson, company K, One Hundred and
    Fifty-Ninth.
George Showers, company E, Third.

FALLS TOWNSHIP.

Samuel Barnet, (colored), Fifty-Fifth United States.
James F. Bell, company G, Ninety-Seventh.
John M. Bell, " G, "
Lewis Coos, company D, One Hundred and Fifty-Ninth.
Hiram Cox, company E, Third.
Henry Cooper, company G, Ninety-Seventh.
David Ivins, colored.
Francis Lewis, company G, Thirty-Second.
William II. Musselman, company E, Third.
John Martin, company G, Ninety-Seventh.
John Rodecker, company G, Ninety-Seventh.
Jeremiah J. Reynolds, " G, "
J. P. Somers, company A, Sixteenth.
Thomas Salisberry, company G, Ninety-Seventh.
Mathew Sellars, " G, "
Alex. Tanner, company D, Thirty-Second.

HIGHLAND TOWNSHIP.

—— Fisher, One Hundred and Sixtieth.
Cephas Hammond, company I, One Hundred and
    Twenty-Second.
Wm. H. Hammond, company A, Fifteenth.
George H. Hanks, company E, Second.
Jasper Halsey, company A, Seventy-Eighth.
George Johns,   "   I,   "
John McCune,   "   F,   "
James F. McGee,   "   A, Fifteenth.
Hamilton I. Miller,   "   A, Seventy-Eighth.
Alfred Shamblin,   "   E, Second.
William Sampson.
Joseph V. Sampson, company F, Seventy-Eighth.
Joseph G. Thompson,   "   A,   "
John H. Trace,   "   A,   "
John R. Wilson,   "   A,   "
Thomas C. Wilson,   "   F,   "

HOPEWELL TOWNSHIP.

James F. Bell, company G, Ninety-Seventh.

Aseph Cooper, " B, Seventy-Eighth.

John Dare, company B, One Hundred and Thirty-Fifth.

Emanuel Drumm, company G, Ninety-Seventh.

Andrew Francis, company A, Seventy-Eighth.

Thomas Gladman, " K, One Hundred and Twenty-Second.

William Hughes, " B, One Hundred and Thirty-Fifth. .

George W. Loy, company B, Seventy-Eighth.

Isaac Leasure, One Hundred and Twenty-Second.

Nelson Lewis, company B, One Hundred and Thirty-Fifth.

Henry Lawyer, company B, One Hundred and Thirty-Fifth.

Henry Leasure, company K, Ninety-Seventh.

John Miller, " C, "

Macajah Martin, " B, One Hundred and Thirty-Fifth.

John McBride, One Hundred and Twenty-Second.

Samuel H. Prior, company G, Thirty-Second.

Anthony M. Prior, " B, One Hundred and Thirty-Fifth.

Leroy Roberts, company B, One Hundred and Thirty-Fifth.

David Sheppard, company B, Seventy-Eighth.

Bazel Storms, " K, Ninety-Seventh.

Lemon B. Stevens, " G, "

David W. Varner, " G, "

Harrison Varner, " B, Seventy-Eighth.

HARRISON TOWNSHIP.

Alfred Anderson, company H, Second West Virginia
 Cavalry.
Daniel Brown, company E, Second.
John Bergarmer,   "   E,   "
John Bowman,   "   E,   "
Sylvester L. Bailey, "   E, Seventy-Eighth.
John Barber,   "   A, Sixty-Second.
Lewis Epley, Fifth Cavalry.
John A. Good, company A, One Hundred and Twenty-
 Second.
William Good, company E, One Hundred and Ninety-
 Fifth.
John Lawson, company E, Second.
James Luman, company A, One Hundred and Twenty-
 Second.
Abraham Leffler, company I, One Hundred and Tenth.
Peter Leffler, company I, Twelfth Cavalry.
Caleb Monroe,   "   E, Ninety-Seventh.
Nicholas Mountz, company A, One Hundred and
 Twenty-Second.
—— Morrison, (unknown.)
George W. Olden, company E, Ninety-Seventh.
Isaiah Poland,   "   E, Second.
James H. Sheppard,   "   E,   "
Jeremiah Sheppard, company I, One Hundred and
 Twenty-Second.
Philip Schaus, company C, Fifteenth.
Charles Sailer, First.

Henry Sulivant, company E, Second.
William Sulivant, " B, Seventy-Eighth.
Jacob Schneider, " E, Third.
Joseph Thompson, " E, Second.
Joseph Trost, company A, One Hundred and Twenty-
Second.
Joseph Trost, company E, One Hundred and Ninety-
Fifth.
William D. Weaver, company E, Ninety-Seventh.
Lewis Young, company E, Second.

JACKSON TOWNSHIP.

Denton Adams, company I, One Hundred and Twenty-Second.

Jasper Adams, company I, One Hundred and Twenty-Second.

Thomas Barker, company D, Sixteenth.

Horace J. Fairall, company II, One Hundred and Fifty-Ninth.

William Griffin, company D, Fifty-First.

Jeremiah Ketchum, company A, Seventy-Sixth.

Ezeriah McVicker, " D, Sixteenth..

George McCann, company F, One Hundred and Twenty-Second.

J. G. Moore, company II, One Hundred and Fifty-Ninth.

Henry Nelson, Seventy-Fifth.

James Parker, company II, One Hundred and Fifty-Ninth.

D. F. Weekly, company A, Seventy-Sixth.

Jacob Whiteman, company I, One Hundred and Twenty-Second.

David Victor, company A, Seventy-Sixth..

John W. Wilson, Seventy-Eighth.

JEFFERSON TOWNSHIP.

Jacob Ane, company F, Ninety-Seventh.
Benjamin W. Barton, company B, First.
James F. Cole, company F, Sixty-Second.
John Cassell,   "   F,   "
Josephus Cordray, company B, Eighteenth.
Annanias Dunn,   "   F, Ninety-Seventh.
James Dwiggins,   "   F, Ninety-Seventh.
James W. Dewar,   "   B, Eighteenth.
Seymour Davis, company B, Eighteenth.
Julius Evans,   "   F, Sixty-Second.
Martin W. Griffee, Ninth Cavalry.
Edward J. Hickey, company D, Sixteenth.
James Holden,   "   D,   "
Jasper Jackson,   "   D,   "
Charles C. Macham,   "   F, Ninety-Seventh.
Hugh McMurry,   "   D, Sixteenth.
Alex. Morton,   "   F, Ninety-Seventh.
David Powell,   "   B, Eightieth.
John V. Shipley,   "   F, Ninety-Seventh.
W. H. H. Sprague, company D, Sixteenth.
Washington Spence,   "   F,   "
Robert Sharpe,   "   F, Sixty-Second.
John Williams,   "   F, Ninety-Seventh.
George Wolford, Tenth Cavalry.
John W. Weaver, company F, Ninety-Seventh.
Adam Yeast,   "   E,   "

LICKING TOWNSHIP.

J. F. Baird, company C, Seventy-Eighth.
Ashuel Bilen, company II, One Hundred Fifty-Ninth.
Mifflin Cusac,   "   B, Thirtieth.
John Estworthy, "   K, Ninety-Seventh.
Lycurgus Drone, "   G,   "
Daniel Diven, Eighteenth United States.
Benjamin Ditter, company H, Thirty-First.
James Gochanour,   "   B, Seventy-Eighth.
John Gochanour,   "   B,   "
Alvah Fleming, company G, One Hundred and Thirty-
     Fifth.
Abel Farnsworth, company B, Seventy-Eighth.
James Musgrove,   "   C, Sixty-Second.
John G. Moore,   "   A, Seventy-Sixth.
John W. Montgomery, company B, Thirtieth.
Willam II. Sullivant,   "   D, Seventy-Eighth.
Charles C. Smart,   "   C, Sixteenth.
Henry Sherman, company G, Ninety-Seventh.
Vincent Staggers,   "   G,   "
James M. Thompson, company B, Seventy-Eighth.
David W. Varner,   "   G, Ninety-Seventh.

MEIGS TOWNSHIP.

Patrick Berry, company A, Sixteenth.

Elisha Crawford, company H, One Hundred and Twenty-Second.

Charles D. Flowers, company C, Seventy-Eighth.

Horace B. Flowers,   "

John Jones,   "   C,   "

John Lyons,   "   A,   "

William Hatton, company F, One Hundred and Twenty-Second.

Martin V. Murphy, company F, One Hundred and Twenty-Second.

Thomas Mitchell, company F, One Hundred and Twenty-Second.

William W. Morris, company H, Sixty-Second.

Hugh K. McRoberts,   "   C, Seventy-Eighth.

Seth Marshall, company F, One Hundred and Twenty-Second.

David Peirce, company C, Seventy-Eighth.

A. B. Sims, company K, One Hundred and Twenty-Second.

Hiram Sims, company F, One Hundred and Twenty-Second.

Joseph R. Starrett, company C, Seventy-Eighth.

James F. Wilson, company F, One Hundred and Twenty-Second.

MONROE TOWNSHIP.

Benjamin Conway, company F, Seventy-Eighth.
William Boal,   "   H, Forty-Seventh.
Tunis Elson,   "   I, Sixty-Ninth.
William L. Elson,   "   I,   "
Samuel T. Morrison, company F, Seventy-Eighth.
John McCune,   "   F,   "
Ezra Ross, company E, Ninety-Seventh.
Perry Sprague, "   F, Seventy-Eighth.
John McFee, company H, Forty-Seventh.
John Robbins,   "   I, Sixty-Ninth.
John Trimble,   "   F, Seventy-Eighth.
Philip Shaffer,   "   F, Seventy-Eighth.

MADISON TOWNSHIP.

John Chadwick, company D, Sixteenth.
David C. Dunmead,   "   D,   "
David A. Gibbons,   "   F, Ninety-Seventh.
Frank Gressell,   "   F, Sixty-Second.
Isaiah F. Kinney,   "   D, Sixteenth.
Thomas Hittle, company I, One Hundred and Twenty-
   Second.
Joseph Parkerson, company F, Sixty-Second.
Robert Seabring, company B, Fourth.
Sylvester Stanley,   "   F, Ninety-Seventh.
Daniel St. Clair,   "   D, Sixteenth.
John St. Clair,   "   F, Ninety-Seventh.
William R. Tudor, company I, One Hundred and
   Twenty-Second.
Andrew Wilson, company F, Ninety-Seventh.
James Whittingham, "   F,   "

MUSKINGUM TOWNSHIP.

Curtis W. Campbell, company G, Ninety-Seventh.
Spencer Fletcher, company D, Sixteenth.
Levi Frost, company B, Fifteenth.
Joshua G. Fletcher, company D, Sixteenth.
George Fletcher, company G, Ninety-Seventh.
John Granger, company F, One hundred and Twenty-
　　Second.
R. W. P, Hunter, company G, Ninety-Seventh.
William James, company I, One Hundred and Twenty-
　　Second.
William H. Madden, company G, Ninety-Seventh.
Henry Moor, company K, One Hundred and Twenty-
　　Second.
James McFarland, company D, Sixteenth.
—— Ortlet, (unknown.)
John St. Clair, company G, Ninety-Seventh.
Charles Tatam, company D, Sixteenth.
George B. Wright, company F, Ninety-Seventh.

NEWTON TOWNSHIP.

C. W. Barrel, company B, Seventy-Eighth.
William Boney, company A, Sixteenth.
W. S. Bowers, company E, Seventy-Eighth.
Moses Bash, company — Seventy-Sixth.
James Cherry, company A, Sixty-Second.
James Edwin, company B, Third.
Martin Gafney, company G, Seventy-Eighth.
Hamline Gardner, company B, Seventy-Eighth.
Daniel Horn, company B, Seventy-Eighth.
Joseph Jenkins, company B, Seventy-Eighth.
Benjamin F. Keys, company G, Thirty-Second.
William Loy, company — Seventy-Eighth.
Charles Night, company B, Seventy-Eighth.
Francis Retallick, company F, One Hundred and Twen-
    ty-Second.
L. A. Roberts, company B, Seventy-Eighth.
George W. Richardson, company B, Seventy-Eighth.
Jacob Smitley, company B, Seventy-Sixth.
David Slack, company A, Sixty-Second.
J. W. Spring, company A, Seventy-Eighth.
Samuel Stansberry, company B, One Hundred and Thir-
    ty-Fifth.

PERRY TOWNSHIP.

Gideon Arnold, Tenth Cavalry.
Isaac Berkhimer, company F, Twenty-Fifth.
George Edwards, Ninth Cavalry.
William Frazier, company F, Seventy-Sixth.
Mitchell Huffman, company — Twenty-Fifth.
John McHunter, company F, Seventy-Eighth.
John Morrison, company F, Seventy-Eighth.
Edward B. McCracken, company F, One Hundred and
    Twenty-Second.
Richard Reed, company E, One Hundred and Eighty-
    Second.
John Stires, company F, One Hundred and Ninety-
    Eighth.
Samuel Shuck, company E, Ninety-Seventh.
Alfred Shamblin.
James Taylor, company F, Seventy-Eighth.
John Wine,   "   F,   "   "

RICH HILL TOWNSHIP.

Ezra Atchinson, company E, One Hundred and Twenty-Second.

James Atchinson, company E, One Hundred and Twenty-Second.

John Bracken, company B, Ninety-Seventh.

E. A. Bain,   "   K,   "   "

John C. Cramblett, "   G,   "   "

Alexander M. Cox, "   A, Seventy-Eighth.

John Crawford,   "   A,   "   "

Henry Crawford,   "   A,   "   "

James Crawford,   "   A,   "   "

C. Z. Dollman, company —, Ninety-Seventh.

Simon Elliott,   "   E, Second.

Hugh Elliott, (1) "   B, Ninety-Seventh.

Hugh Elliott, (2) "   B,   "   "

John Foster,   "   E, One Hundred and Twenty-Second.

Lewis Forsythe, company A, Fifteenth.

James Fleming, company A, Seventy-Eighth.

John Hoop, (unknown.)

John Humble, company B, Ninety-Seventh.

Samuel Jones, company D, Seventy-Eighth.

Benoni Leadman, company A, Fifteenth.

D. B. Monroe, company A, Sixty-Second.

James L. Polen, company —, Ninety-Seventh.

Abraham Pollock, company H, One Hundred and Twenty-Sixth.

Richard Stephens, company E, One Hundred and Twenty-Second.

Joseph Wilson, company A, Seventy-Eighth.

SALEM TOWNSHIP.

Frederick Aler, company I, One Hundred and **Twenty-**
Second.
Alva Bartholemew, company E, Ninety-Seventh.
William II. Bowden,   "   "   "   "
Samuel A. Brill, (unknown.)
Sutherland Baughman, company A, Sixteenth.
Ezra Baughman, company —, Fifteenth.
George Bowman, company E, Ninety-Seventh.
Henry II. Doughty, company E, Ninety-Seventh.
Jasper Daily, company —, Fifteenth.
James II. Forrest, company E, Ninety-Seventh.
Asa Henry, Thirteenth Tennessee.
Charles Keys, company E, Ninety-Seventh.
John McDowell, company C, Sixty-Second.
John Oliver, company F, Seventy-Eighth.
Homer II. Roff, Marine.
Converse M. Shirer, company E, Ninety-Seventh.
Benjamin F. Shirer, Fourth Cavalry.
Asa Vernon, company K, Sixty-Fourth.
Nicholas Vernon, company F, Seventy-Eighth.

SALT CREEK TOWNSHIP.

John A. Armstrong, company D, Seventy-Eighth.
William Allen, company —,   "   "
C. W. Bailey, company A, Fifteenth.
James II. Crumbaker, company E, Third.
Manly Crumbaker, company D, Seventy-Eighth.
Samuel P. Campbell, company D,   "   "
John E. Harkness, company G, Ninety-Seventh.
Abel F. Kille, Gun Boat.   •
J. F. Mathews, company —, Seventy-Eighth.
Benjamin Matson, company —,   "   "
John F. Moore, company B,   "   "
Hiram Mercer, company, —,   "   "
William Sutton, company B,   "   "
Charles Smith, company —, One Hundred and Fifty-
    Ninth.
Lewis Vogt, company A, Seventy-Eighth.

SPRINGFIELD TOWNSHIP.

Randolph C. Aston, company B, Seventy-Eighth.
F. M. Atkinson, company B, Twenty-Fourth.
James Atkinson, company E, Nineteenth.
Henry Alwes, company II, Seventy-Eighth.
J. W. Aston, company E, Nineteenth.
Henry Beaty, (colored) company M, Fifth U. S.
George Brown,   "   "   "   "   "
William Berkshire, company K, Ninety-Seventh.
William A. Cocerel, company —, Twelfth.
John L. Chapman, company K, Ninety-Seventh.
William Crooks, company B, One Hundred and Thirty-
    Fifth.
Richard Dickerson, company B, Seventy-Eighth.
Thomas Dorsey, company —, First.
John Davey, company E, Nineteenth.
William Deitrick, company A, Sixty-Second.
William Emery, company D,   "   "
Robert Figley, company B, Seventy-Eighth.
Howard C. France, company E, Nineteenth.
Western Fletcher, (colored) M, Eleventh U. S.
John Gray, company C, Fortieth.
William Gardner, company K, Ninety-Seventh.
Miles D. Gadd, company E, Nineteenth.
Lieut. Thomas Hopes, company F, Seventy-Eighth.
M. K. Hawkins, Seventy-Eighth.
Nathaniel Hall, (colored) company M, Eleventh U. S.
Finley Hemphill, company K, Ninety-Seventh.
John W. Harding, company E, Nineteenth.
Lewis P. Haver, company E, Third.

John Hafthill, Eleventh U. S.
Greenberry Honeycut, (col'd) company D, Eleventh U. S.
Alvah James, company C, Thirteenth Cavalry.
Alfred Joselyn, company —, One Hundred and Twen-
ty-Second.
William Kinney, (colored) company M, Eleventh U. S.
Charles Koontz, company E, Nineteenth.
James Kelly, Gunboat.
Samuel Lewis, company B, Seventy-Eighth.
James Lewis,   "   "   "   "
George H. Mathews,   "   "   "
Wm. McMillan, (unknown) Andersonville Prison.
Joseph Osmond,   "   "   "
George I. Potts, Q. M. Sergeant, Ninety-Fifth.
J. W. Palmer, company —, Nineteenth.
John Phillips, company —, Twenty-Fourth.
Joel Runnion, company F, Seventy-Eighth.
Major B. C. G. Reed, One Hundred and Seventy-Fourth.
Horace Rheynolds, company —, Seventy-Sixth,
Albert Smith, company B, Seventy-Eighth.
John W. Saladee, company G, Ninety-Seventh.
Charles Smith, company C, Thirteenth Cavalry.
Catharinus Springer, company E, Nineteenth.
John Skinner, company B, Seventy-Eighth.
Robert Stockdale, company K, Ninety-Seventh.
B. F. Scott, company K, Ninety-Seventh.
Warren B. Schnebly, company —, Second Cavalry.
John H. Spalding, company K, Ninety-Seventh.
Thomas Starts, (colored) company —, Fifth U. S.
Austin Tuttle, company A, Sixteenth.
John Thompson, (colored) unknown.
William Harrison Wiles, company B, Fifteenth.
Cordon R. Wiles, company B, Seventy-Eighth.
Benoni A. Williams, Thirteenth Cavalry.
Charles Weaver, company E, Nineteenth.
John Weaver, company B, Seventy-Eighth.

UNION TOWNSHIP.

William Asher, One Hundred and Twenty-Second.
Joseph Alexander, Forty-Sixth.
Nealy Alexander, Forty-Sixth.
James Alexander, company A, Fifteenth.
Samuel Barnett, (Libby) company F, Twenty-Sixth.
W. L. Brown, Fifteenth.
R. M. Brown, company A, Fifteenth.
Captain J. C. Cummins, company A, Fifteenth.
Lieutenant James T. Caldwell, Seventy-Eighth.
William S. Caldwell, company I, One Hundred and
    Twenty-Second.
Lieutenant Philip Gibbons, Seventy-Eighth.
James Gormley, company A, Fifteenth.
Captain Thomas N. Hanson, company A, Fifteenth.
Lieutenant Andrew L. Hadden, "   A,   "
Cephas Hammond, company I, One Hundred and
    Twenty-Second.
James L. Hadden, company A, Fifteenth.
Samuel Hurrell,   "   F, Seventy-Eighth.
Robert Hanson, Seventy-Eighth.
Levi Hammond,   "
Samuel W. Hughes,   "
Jefferson O. McMillan, company I, One Hundred and
    Twenty-Second.
James F. McGee, company A, Fifteenth.
E. E. Madden,   "   A,   "
William Price,   "   A,   "

David McCutcheon, company A, Fifteenth.
Theo. Reasoner, Seventy-Eighth.
George F. Richey, company A, Seventy-Eighth.
T. W. Skinner, company A, Fifteenth.
John F. Timms, company I, One Hundred and Twenty-
    Second.
Stephen W. Van Kirk, company I, One Hundred and
    Twenty-Second.
John McWhirter, company A, Seventy-Eighth.
Wesley West, company F, Seventy-Eighth.
Alonzo Wilson, company A, Fifteenth.
Jonathan Whitiker, company F, Seventy-Eighth.
Lewis Williams, Eighty-Eighth.
Harvey White, company A, Fifteenth.

WASHINGTON TOWNSHIP.

Noah Colcier, company F, One Hundred and Eighty-
Third.

George Dunn, One Hundred and Fifty-Ninth.

James L. Dunn, company F. One Hundred and Twenty-
Second.

Henry Fulton, (unknown.)

Francis Godfrey, company D, Seventy-Eighth.

George Herald, company E, Nineteenth.

Charles Wm. Kaemmerer, company A, Seventy-Eighth.

Charles Little, company F, One Hundred and Twenty-
Second.

William Monyghan, company K, Seventy-Eighth.

Joseph Morgan, Tenth Cavalry.

Henry Sutton, company K, Seventy-Eighth.

Jacob W. Wright, company K, One Hundred and
Twenty-Second.

WAYNE TOWNSHIP.

Jeptha R. Austin, company E, Second.

Jacob Dietenback, company A, One Hundred and Twenty-Second.

John Engleheart, company A, Sixteenth.

Thomas Fulkerson, company A, One Hundred and Twenty-Second.

E. M. Harding, One Hundred and Seventy-Eighth.

George W. Irvin, company A, Seventy-Eighth.

Absalom Krewson, company A, One Hundred and Twenty-Second.

James Luman, company A, One Hundred and Twenty-Second.

John F. McMillen, company A, One Hundred and Twenty-Second.

William Norris, Seventy-Eighth.

Jeremiah Norris,   "   "

Jacob G. Schnider, Third.

George W. Settle, company F, Seventy-First.

Samuel Scott, company A, Sixteenth.

Francis M. Story, company F, Seventy-Eighth.

Oliver C. Story, company F, Seventy-Eighth.

Samuel Shuck, company E, Ninety-Seventh.

Andrew Voll, company A, One Hundred and Twenty-Second.

A. W. Williamson, One Hundred and Twenty-Second.

Walter I. Wells, company A, One Hundred and Twenty-Second.

David E. Watson, One Hundred and Twenty-Second.

Jacob Withers, company A, Seventy-Eighth.

ZANESVILLE—FIRST WARD.

John F. Carlow, (unknown.)
James Eoff, company G, Thirty-Second.
Barnhard Fix, company E, Third.
Narvil Greenland, Nineteenth.
Frank Greenland, Twenty-Fourth.
Capt. John C. Hazlett, company H, Second.
Lieut. Charles E. Hazlett, company D, Fifth Reg. Art.
Enoch Hedges, company E, Second.
Henderson Jordon, company C, Seventy-Eighth.
William Monroe, company A, One Hundred and Twen-
    ty-Second.
John Morrison, company A, Sixteenth.
Lieut. Joshua Madden, First Artillery.
George Morrison, company A, Second
—— Owens, company I, One Hundred and Ninety-Fifth.

ZANESVILLE—SECOND WARD.

B. Compton, company A, Sixteenth.

Jacob Christman, company A, Ninth Cavalry.

John Cantwell, company C, Seventy-Eighth.

Patrick Cantwell, Eighteenth U. S.

J. Morton Dillon, company E, Ninety-Seventh.

Edward English, company C, Seventy-Eighth.

J. H. Horseman, company B, Sixty-Second.

Gordon Huntingdon, company A, One Hundred and Twenty-Second.

B. H. Jordon, company C, Seventy-Eighth,

Lewis C. Jordon.

John R. Johnston, company E, Second.

James Morton, company C, Seventy-Eighth.

George W. Newell, company F, One Hundred and Twenty-Second.

Isaac Priest, company K, Nineteenth.

Francis Porter, company G, Seventy-Eighth.

Cyrus Sarchett, company A, One Hundred and Twenty-Second.

Robert J. Tirrel, (colored) Eleventh U. S.

Owen Sullivan, Seventy-Eighth.

Arthur J. Van Horne, company F, Ninety-Fifth.

D. C. Willis, company I, Seventy-Eighth.

ZANESVILLE—THIRD WARD.

Alexander Buble, company A, Sixteenth.
Alexander Christy, company A, Sixteenth.
Jacob Cushman, Eighth.
Lieut. J. Stanly Cochran, Nineteenth.
William Flowers, One Hundred and Seventy-Eighth.
John Hyatt, company E, Second.
John Knawer, company K, One Hundred and Twenty-
    Second.
Joseph Keller, company F, One Hundred and Twenty-
    Second.
Adgt. Dan C. Liggett, Sixty-Second.
David Mercer, company H, Second.
H. Pigram, company H, Second.
Samuel Reynolds, (unknown.)
Walter Roderick, Gunboat.
George C. Shuback, company B, First O. Cavalry.
Jacob Voct, company E, Tenth Cavalry.
Leander Williams, company A, Sixteenth.
Charles Wilson, (colored) Fifth U. S.

ZANESVILLE FOURTH WARD.

Joseph Anderson, company K, Seventy-Eighth.

William Arthur, company D, Sixty-Second.

Thomas Bellville, company F, One Hundred and Twenty Second.

William Blixenschultz, company F, Seventy-Eighth.

Moses Bash, company D, Seventy-Eighth.

Jasper Cochran, company A, One Hundred and Twenty-Second.

Newton Cockerell, company A, One Hundred and Twenty-Second.

Hyram Cowan, company E, Second.

George Fridoline, company E, Ninety-Seventh.

Thomas Grisby, company H, Seventeenth.

Edward H. Hilliard, company I, One Hundred and Twenty-Second.

George Hawn, company K, Sixty-Second.

John T. Hainess, company B, Tenth Cavalry.

William Laughlin, Seventy-Eighth.

Wesley M. Lyons, company A, Seventy-Eighth.

John McMulkin, company A, Seventy-Eighth.

David Maas, company E, Second.

Valentine Mummel, company E, Nineteenth.

James Male, company I, Sixty-Seventh.

Thomas H. Parkinson, company E, Nineteenth.

Thomas Passwater, company F, Sixty-Second.

John Robinson, company E, Ninety-Seventh.

Christian Rines, Twenty-Fourth.

Henry Ratliff, (unknown.)

James Stull, company I, One Hundred and Twenty-Second.

Ugene Sulivant, Twenty-Fourth. .

Hiram Sears, company F, One Hundred and Twenty-Second.

James H. Smith, company A, Sixteenth.

Cyrus Sarchet, company A, One Hundred and Twenty-Second.

Alexander Winn, Twenty-Fourth.

J. M. Winn, company F, Seventy-Eighth.

James Wray, Heavy Artillery.

John Young, company F, One Hundred and Twenty-Second.

DECEASED OFFICERS.

Major William Edwards, Sixty-Second.
Major B. G. O. Reed, One Hundred and Seventy-Fourth.
Captain E. Hillis Talley, company D, Seventy-Eighth.
    "   Thomas L. Hanson, company A, Fifteenth.
    "   William Berkshire, company K, Ninety-Seventh.
    "   John C. Hazelett, company E, Second.
    "   J. C. Cummins, Fifteenth.
Adjutant Dan C. Liggett, Sixty-Second.
Lieut. Thomas Hopes, company F, Seventy-Eighth.
    "   Charles E. Hazelett, company D, Fifth Artillery.
    "   Hamline Gardner, company B, Seventy-Eighth.
    "   John T. Caldwell, Seventy-Eighth.
    "   William Gardner, company K, Ninety-Seventh.
    "   Joshua Madden, First Artillery.
    "   Edward H. Hilliard. company I, One Hundred
        and Twenty-Second.
    "   Frederick Lentz. company K, Nineteenth.
    "   J. Stanly Cochran, Nineteenth.
    "   Jefferson O. McMillen, company I, One Hundred
        and Twenty-Second.
    "   Andrew L. Hadden, company A, Fifteenth.

ERRATA.

It is stated on page four, that the entire number of deaths by battle, in this roll, is five hundred and eighty-four. At the time of preparing the form for the press, containing the above page and number, it was correct as far as known, but an accurate count at the close of this form, gives the whole number at six hundred and one. Number of officers, nineteen.